Lonely Wolf Pup

Susan Hughes

Illustrations by Heather Graham

SCHOLASTIC CANADA LTD.
Toronto New York London Auckland Sydney
Mexico City New Delhi Hong Kong Buenos Aires

Scholastic Canada Ltd.
604 King Street West, Toronto, Ontario M5V 1E1, Canada

Scholastic Inc.
557 Broadway, New York, NY 10012, USA

Scholastic Australia Pty Limited
PO Box 579, Gosford, NSW 2250, Australia

Scholastic New Zealand Limited
Private Bag 94407, Greenmount, Auckland, New Zealand

Scholastic Children's Books
Euston House, 24 Eversholt Street, London NW1 1DB, UK

National Library of Canada Cataloguing in Publication

Hughes, Susan, 1960-
Lonely wolf pup / Susan Hughes ; illustrations by Heather Graham.

(Wild paws)
Originally publ. 2003.

ISBN 978-0-545-98527-7

I. Graham, Heather II. Title. III. Series : Hughes, Susan, 1960- . Wild paws.
PS8565.U42L65 2009   jC813'.54   C2009-901188-3

ISBN-10 0-545-98527-7

6 5 4 3 2 1   Printed in Canada   09 10 11 12 13 14

To my sweet daughter, Georgia.

Thank you to Jody and Dale Gienow of the Muskoka Wildlife Centre for lending their expertise and helpful suggestions to this story.

Contents

Chapter One

Animal Lovers

Max kicked the colourful, dry leaves on the ground. She loved the scrunchy sound that the brittle leaves made in autumn.

"I can't believe it," she said to her friend Sarah. "Can you?"

Sarah looked up. "Believe what?" she asked. She tucked her bare hands into her jeans pockets to keep them warm.

"Today's Saturday. And Halloween is Tuesday. It will be here in just a few days!" Max exclaimed. "I can hardly believe it's nearly November. Just look. Bandit and Flora are really getting chubby."

"That's for sure," agreed Sarah. "They've been

packing in the food for weeks now!"

The two girls were at the Wild Paws and Claws Clinic and Rehabilitation Centre — again. They spent a lot of time helping out there. Abigail Abernathy, the centre's director, counted on them. The girls had been there almost every day that past summer. Since school had begun, they'd been volunteering two afternoons a week and every Saturday.

Max and Sarah stood in front of a large enclosure, watching the two raccoons. They both had salt-and-pepper coats and black masks across their faces. But they were easy to tell apart. Bandit was the larger one, and he was missing an eye. Flora was smaller, and the claws on her hind legs were damaged. Some of the wild animals that came to the centre only needed to stay a short time. Then they were released back into the wilderness. But Bandit and Flora couldn't survive on their own. They were long-time residents at Wild Paws and Claws.

Sarah giggled. "I don't know if these roly-poly big eaters will fit in their dens!"

Max looked at the hole in the hollow tree that stood in the corner of the enclosure. "I know. As Bandit gets larger and larger, that hole looks smaller and smaller. And look," she pointed toward the other corner of the enclosure. There were several

rocks there that formed a natural protected crevice. "Flora's den is full of dead leaves. She's going to have to suck in her tummy to fit inside there!"

Sarah's blue eyes sparkled as she laughed. Then she glanced at the raccoons' almost empty water container. "We'll have to come back soon to fill up their pan," she said.

Max nodded. A wonderful feeling spread through her. She felt so lucky. Who would have believed that she – Max Kearney, animal lover – would become a helper at a wildlife centre? Caring for injured wild animals was like a dream come true!

Max and her family had only lived in Maple Hill a few months. But now it was hard for her to remember life before Wild Paws and Claws. She remembered how nervous she had been when she'd first arrived in town. She had been anxious about making a new friend.

But then Max had found an orphaned baby bobcat while hiking on a nearby trail, and the adventure had begun! It led her to the rehabilitation centre, where Tuffy the bobcat was now recovering. And it had helped her to meet Sarah, her new best friend.

Max and Sarah continued on to the red squirrel's enclosure. Max peeked in and spotted saucy Nutcracker. Many of the animals at Wild Paws and

Claws were starting to grow their winter coats. In the summer, the red squirrel had sported an orangey coat with a white belly outlined in black. Now, Nutcracker had a red back to match her red tail, and her white belly had turned to grey. The black line of fur was gone altogether.

The blind squirrel heard the girls and began nattering at them loudly. He stood protectively in front of a pile of pinecones.

"Oh, don't worry, Nutcracker," Max called. "We won't steal your cones!"

"Yeah, redhead. We're the ones that gave them to you, remember?" added Sarah. She wagged one of her own red braids at the squirrel.

Over the last week, the girls had searched for clusters of pinecones in the surrounding woods. Then they had scattered them here and there in the squirrel's enclosure. Nutcracker had immediately gotten busy. He had picked out a special spot in the rear of his pen. Using his sense of smell, he had collected the pinecones and placed them there in a heap. Abigail, or Abbie for short, had explained that Nutcracker would eat the seeds from the cones during the long winter.

Ch-ch-ch-ch, replied Nutcracker loudly. He stood his ground beside the pile of pinecones.

5

"He doesn't believe us," laughed Sarah.

"OK, well, we'll be gone in a minute," Max assured him. She waved the sheets of paper she was holding. "Let's take care of these, Sarah. We told Abbie we'd do it before we finished today."

"OK," Sarah agreed.

Abbie Abernathy owned Wild Paws and Claws. At her clinic, she worked hard to see that injured animals recovered and were returned to the wild.

Abbie had been in the office all afternoon, trying to find bargain prices for food and supplies. Running a wildlife clinic with very little money was difficult. In fact, when Max and Sarah had first met Abbie, the clinic had been in danger of closing.

But the two determined girls had come up with a great idea: they would organize an open house at the centre. Thanks to their hard work, the event was a success. They had raised enough money to keep the clinic open – and the animals safe – for some time to come.

There were two torn information sheets posted in front of Nutcracker's enclosure. Last weekend, Max and Sarah had prepared new sheets about the red squirrel. Max had added drawings of two other squirrel species that could be found in the area: the grey squirrel and the northern flying squirrel.

The girls took down the old, weather-worn papers. Sarah held each of the new information sheets in place while Max stapled them. They covered the sheets with clear plastic to keep out the rain and snow.

"There you go, Nutcracker," Sarah called. "Visitors can read all about you once again!"

"Come on. We'd better head back to the office. It's starting to get dark," said Max.

The girls said goodbye to the chittering squirrel and hurried along the leafy path that led from the enclosures to the main office building.

"What are you going to be for Halloween?" Max asked Sarah.

"I'm going to be a witch. What about you?" Sarah replied.

"I'm going to be a . . . "

Suddenly the girls froze.

Aooooo! . . . Aooooo!

"What's that?" Sarah said, nervously. "It sounds like a — "

Aooooo! . . . Aooooo!

Sarah clutched Max's arm. "That sounds like a wolf!" she cried. "I'm scared!"

Then, all of a sudden, it was right there on the path in front of them.

Chapter Two

A Halloween Joke

"*Aooooo!*"

The wolf stood on the path in front of the girls. It had two legs and was dressed in black. Its face was hairy, with large white teeth and red eyes. Its paws were hairy too, with long white claws.

"David," Max scolded her brother. "That wasn't very nice."

The wolf put its head back and howled again.

"*Aooooo!*"

Sarah released her grip on Max's arm. "David?" She took a deep breath. "Oh, boy, you scared me," she said shakily. "I'm afraid of wolves. Real ones, that is."

David pulled his mask up. He looked a little ashamed. "Oh, sorry, I guess," he said. "It was just a pre-Halloween joke."

Max rolled her eyes at him and frowned.

"Max? That you?"

"Hello, Sarah!" Two voices came from near the office building. In the fading light, Max could see her Grandma waving. Sarah's mother stood beside her. It was pick-up time. The kids waved back and headed over to them.

"Grandma was on her way to get you," David said. "I was trying on my costume, and I thought this might be a good way to test it out," he added sheepishly. He poked at Sarah. "So I really scared you?"

"Yeah, you did," Sarah assured him with a shiver. "There's something . . . I don't know, something scary about wolves."

Max looked at Sarah curiously. "You're scared of wolves? For real?"

"Sure, everyone is," Sarah said. "They're big and they have big teeth. And they eat people."

Max's brown eyes opened wide. "*Eat* people?"

"Well, just look at David's costume," Sarah pointed out. "Teeth, claws . . . scary. Haven't you heard of the Wolf Man? Haven't you heard of werewolves?"

Max noticed Sarah glancing nervously toward the trees as they walked. "Yes," Max said slowly. "But the Wolf Man and werewolves aren't real. They're just made up."

"Well, that's still one animal that I wouldn't want anything to do with. In fact, I remember my dad saying that there were wolves around here when he was a boy. They used to live in the forests around Maple Hill." Sarah's eyes darted to the shadowy woods again. "But they're not here anymore."

"Wow," breathed David. "What happened to them?" He scratched at his head with one huge, hairy wolf paw.

Sarah thought for a moment and then shrugged. "I'm not sure," she said. Then she shuddered. "I'm just glad they're gone."

Max couldn't believe her ears. She had thought Sarah loved *all* wild animals. "Sarah, I'm sure you're wrong about wolves. I don't know that much about them, but I think we should find out the facts," Max said. "I'm sure wolves aren't really as scary as you think."

"I don't know," Sarah said with a shiver. "Maybe we could just forget about it for now. Until after Halloween, anyway."

Max didn't want to forget about it. How could Sarah be glad that the wild wolves were gone from Maple Hill?

But Max didn't get the chance to say anything more. Sarah had caught up to her mother and they were heading to their car. "See you at school on Monday," Sarah called to Max.

"OK, Sarah," Max called back. She watched Sarah's car drive away in the growing darkness. It passed a pick-up truck going the other way.

"Is everything all right with Sarah?" Grandma asked, with concern. "She seemed very anxious to get going."

"She's fine," Max said. "I guess."

Max bit her lip. There had to be a way to convince Sarah that wolves weren't awful and scary. She *knew* she could do it somehow.

Just then, the pick-up truck pulled into the driveway of Wild Paws and Claws. It drove right up to the parking lot. It was so dark now that Max couldn't even guess the colour of the truck.

"Oops." Max shook her head. "It's too late for visitors. Maybe Abbie forgot to put out the *Closed* sign."

She began to walk toward the truck, but she felt Grandma's hand on her arm.

"Wait, Max," Grandma said.

Max stopped. "Why?"

But Grandma didn't answer. Now Max realized that the truck engine was still running. She could just make out the shape of a young man jumping out of the truck. He seemed to have his jacket hood pulled around his face. Then someone smaller got out of the passenger seat — a girl wearing a flowing cape and a vampire mask!

The pair hurried to the back of the truck. Max heard the truck's tailgate drop down with a clatter. She could hear the teenager murmuring to the vampire. They seemed to be lifting a large object out of the truck. Yes. Now she could hear them groaning, and she saw that they were setting the bulky shape on the ground.

Just then, the light outside the office came on, and a tall woman with owlish glasses and long, skinny legs flung open the office door. She quickly craned her neck this way and that. It was Abbie, the owner of Wild Paws and Claws.

"Who's there?" she called.

"Friends," called back the hooded teen.

Max heard the tailgate bang shut, and then the teenager and the small vampire disappeared back into the truck. In a moment, the pick-up was speeding away.

Then Max saw the beam of Abbie's flashlight bouncing toward them across the yard. Dust and leaves swirled and whirled around. Max held her breath.

"What is that? What did they leave here?" David asked in a soft, nervous voice.

Then, Abbie was beside them. The beam of her flashlight froze. In its light, across the yard, was a large object shaped like a box. It was about as high as Max's chest and as wide as her stretched-out arms. It was wrapped in a canvas sheet.

Max sucked in her breath. What was it?

"Let's go and investigate," Abbie said calmly. She strode forward, her long legs stretching ahead and her arms sawing back and forth. She hadn't bothered to put on a jacket.

Max and David hurried forward too, with Grandma right behind them.

Max was bursting with curiosity. What could it be? And why had the young people who'd left it here been so secretive?

"Is it a big box?" David asked. "Why would anyone leave a big box?"

But Abbie put up one hand, asking for silence. For a moment, the four of them stood quietly over the mysterious object.

Suddenly Max heard a sound coming from underneath the canvas.

Scritch, scritch, scritch.

"There's something alive in there," Max breathed. Maybe it was an animal — an animal in a crate.

"Let's find out," Abbie said quickly. "Let's get this canvas tarpaulin off first."

A rope was wrapped around the canvas sheet, holding it in place. It was knotted in several places.

"Everyone find a knot to work on," Max urged. Her fingers were cold, but she forced them to pick away at one tight knot and then another.

"I've done the ones on this side," announced Grandma.

"And I'm almost done these," mumbled David.

In a few moments, they were able to loosen the rope and unwrap it from the canvas.

"OK. Max, you lift that side and I'll lift this side," Abbie instructed. "David, please hold the flashlight."

Together Abbie and Max lifted the canvas and began to roll it back.

Max had expected to find a crate underneath. But right away, she realized she had been wrong.

"It's a cage!" cried David.

Abbie corrected him gently. "Not exactly. It's a trap."

Chapter Three

To the
people at
wild paws
and claws

A Trap!

A trap!

Max sucked in her breath. She couldn't believe it. She had never seen a trap before. It did look a lot like a cage, but the sides were covered in a tight wire mesh.

"You see the door?" Abbie pointed out in a low voice. "Bait is put in the trap and the door is raised. When the animal enters the trap and steps on a pan at the back, it triggers the door to spring shut. The door closes on an angle and locks."

Max swallowed hard. She hated the idea of any wild animal being caught against its will.

"OK, Max, let's get a look at what we have in

here. Let's pull the canvas back slowly, so we don't frighten our new visitor," Abbie suggested. "And David, shine the light off to the side so that we can see, but so that the light doesn't shine directly onto the animal or into its eyes."

Max and Abbie rolled the canvas back little by little. More and more of the steel wire mesh was visible.

And then, there it was. Max saw a dark shape pressed into the back of the trap. *What kind of animal was it?*

David moved the flashlight beam a little closer to the trap and a little closer still. "It's a dog!" he cried. "It looks a bit like a German shepherd!"

"Oh, it's a sweet one — a young fellow!" Grandma's crooning voice came from close behind Max. "But it's so skinny!"

Max gasped with concern. The animal *was* skinny, and it was scared. It was crouching low against the steel mesh. It did look like a dog. It had large pointy ears, a narrow muzzle and bristly tan and brown hair.

But for some reason, Max knew it wasn't a dog.

Maybe it was the tail. It seemed a little too bushy. Maybe it was the body. It seemed a little too narrow. Maybe it was the look in the animal's yellow eyes.

It wasn't a dog. Suddenly, Max knew what it must be.

"It's a wolf," she said softly.

David turned and stared at his sister in surprise. His wolf mask was still pushed up on his head.

"Good for you, Max," Abbie said proudly. "You're right. It *is* a wolf, a young one."

Max hadn't taken her eyes off the frightened creature. Now his ears were pressed flat against his head. He looked up at the faces looking in at him and growled uncertainly.

"Is he hurt?" Max asked, with concern. "Do you think that's why he was left here?"

Abbie took off her glasses. Now Max could see the tall woman's worried look. "He certainly looks like he hasn't eaten in a while." Then her face cleared. "But he doesn't seem to be injured," she continued. "That's the one good thing about this type of trap. It catches the animal alive and unhurt."

Max smiled in relief and clasped her hands together. "So we won't need to find a vet." The centre had been without a veterinarian since its long-time volunteer, Dr. Jacobs, had retired.

"But we do need to move him out of this trap and into a larger pen," said Abbie, calmly. "Let's

put the canvas back over him as we prepare to do that. He'll feel more secure that way."

"Can we look at him one more time first?" Max asked.

Abbie smiled. She took the flashlight from David and shone it toward the trap. The wolf pup was standing at the back. When he saw the light, his ears pricked forward curiously. But then they lay flat against his head again. He whined. Max saw his tongue come out and lick at his nose.

Max felt her heart lurch. No wild animal belonged in a trap.

As Abbie and Max replaced the canvas and wrapped the rope around it, a cold wind began to blow. Leaves blew down from the trees. It was almost completely dark.

Even so, something pinned to the underside of the canvas caught Max's eye. It was a piece of paper.

"Look!" she exclaimed. "I think it's a note!"

Quickly Abbie and Max secured the rope, and the group moved closer to the office building, where the outdoor light shone.

"Read it aloud," urged David.

"*To the people at Wild Paws and Claws,*" read Max. "*We found this young wolf in a trap near our farm. Some people around here don't like wolves. They say wolves kill their sheep. We were afraid the trappers might hurt this wolf. We didn't know what to do. So we snuck it onto our truck and brought it to you. Please, please, take care of it.*"

Grandma asked, "Who signed the note? It looked like a teenager and a child who brought it here."

"The note isn't signed," Max said. She turned over the paper. Nothing. Her heart was thumping.

"I guess that's why those young people didn't want anyone to know who they were," Grandma said thoughtfully. "It was someone else's trap that they took."

Abbie shook her head. "I guess they didn't know who to trust. They didn't want to get in trouble for taking the trap. They must have been too scared to even let *us* know who they were."

Max looked at Abbie. "But what if they hadn't taken the trap? What would the trappers have done?" she asked. "Might they really have hurt the wolf — or killed it?" She shuddered. "You know, Sarah was telling me that some people are scared of wolves. They think they eat *people*! Sarah's scared of wolves too."

Abbie shook her head. She put her hand on Max's shoulder. "Wolves definitely don't eat people," she said. "Like most animals, if they feel threatened, they will try to defend themselves. But mainly they are shy. They want to stay away from people."

"And what about killing sheep, like the note says?" David asked.

"Well, they *will* kill sheep or cows, but it's not common. Wolves must eat to survive. They're carnivores, so they prey on animals. They will eat small ones, such as hares, muskrats and raccoons, but they prefer to band together and hunt larger animals, like deer, moose, elk, caribou and beaver. Sometimes the animals they eat disappear from the territory where the wolves live. This can happen because of a natural cause, like a fire or a flood. Or it can happen because of something that humans do, such as cutting down a forest."

Max was listening closely. She nodded to show Abbie that she understood.

"If the food that the wolves normally eat disappears, they might look for something else to eat. Sometimes the wolves will hunt sheep or cattle because they can't find anything else!" Abbie explained. "But it really doesn't happen very often. Wolves will usually move to another place to find the food that they need to survive."

Max looked toward the crate. She thought

about the thin wolf pup with his gangly legs. He'd certainly looked hungry. Max knew that wolves travel in packs, so she guessed he was probably lonely too.

"So, where did this pup come from?" David asked. "How did it end up in a trap near here?"

Max spoke up. "Sarah said that there used to be a wolf pack around Maple Hill. Maybe it's come back."

"I think you're right, Max," said Grandma. "A few days ago, I overheard a man at the grocery-store checkout speaking to the cashier. He lives on a farm north of here. He and his family have seen wolf tracks in the mud near their creek."

Abbie smiled. "Yes, there was a wolf pack near here that vanished a few years ago. Perhaps it has come back, or perhaps this is a new one." Her face clouded over. "But it worries me that anyone around here is trying to trap wolves!"

"Me too," agreed Max. If only Sarah were here. If only she could see this wolf . . . If only she could hear what Abbie had told them . . .

Suddenly Max's face lit up. She snapped her fingers. "You know what?" she said with a grin. Her brown eyes twinkled. "I think I have an idea that might help."

Chapter Four

Home for Now

"What is it? What is it?" begged David, tugging at his sister's arm.

"It's a secret for now," Max said. "I need to talk it over with Sarah first."

David frowned.

"Come on, Max and David," Abbie called. "In the meantime, let's see how we can make our new friend comfortable for the night." She wrapped her arms around her thin body and shivered. "First, I'm going back to the office to get my jacket, and I'll get a few large flashlights as well. Max, could you and David get the trolley?"

Max nodded, and she and her brother took

Abbie's smaller flashlight and headed to the utility shed.

The trolley was like a large wagon without any sides. "Here, jump on," Max offered. "Shine the light ahead of me so I can see where I'm going." Max began pulling the trolley back to the yard, with David riding on top.

"What do you think we should name the wolf?" called David. "Maybe Fangs." He slipped his mask down over his face and waved his hairy paw. "Or Werey the Werewolf."

Max grinned. "I don't think so."

She pictured the young wolf again, with his too-big paws and his almost-grown-up face. She thought of him whimpering sadly. He was so alone. He needed to get back to his family, to the other members of his pack.

"I think I know a good name," Max said. They were almost back to the parking lot. She could see Abbie and Grandma in the light of Abbie's large flashlight. "I think we should call him Solo, because he's all alone."

"Solo," said David, trying it out. "Good idea, sis." Then he called to the others, "Grandma, Abbie, Max wants to name the wolf Solo."

Everyone agreed it was a good name. Then

David took the other large flashlight to light up the area as Abbie, Grandma and Max heaved the trap onto the trolley.

Max couldn't help worrying about the wolf. She knew Solo must be very anxious. First, he had been caught in a trap. Then he had been loaded onto a truck. Now he was being lifted onto a trolley. She thought she could hear whimpering from under the canvas.

"Careful," Max told the others.

Then she leaned into the side of the trap and whispered softly, "It's OK, boy. You'll be out of here soon."

They carefully wheeled the trolley and its cargo along the path toward the enclosure area.

"We'll put him here, as far from the other pens as possible. We'll put up a rope that advises visitors not to come near. Because Solo is a wild animal, he should be kept away from people as much as possible," Abbie reminded them. "We don't want him to get used to us. We want him to keep a healthy fear of people!"

As they stopped in front of the pen that Abbie had pointed to, David asked, "If Solo isn't hurt, why can't we just let him go free?"

"This young wolf knows a lot about hunting.

He knows a lot about how to look after himself. But most wolves, especially young ones, live in packs. We will let him go, and the sooner the better! But we need to make sure we release him in a place where he can find his family again," Abbie explained.

"But how can we do that?" Max asked. "We don't know where he was trapped. And we can't ask the people who brought him here. We don't know who they are."

Abbie shook her head. "You're right, Max." She shrugged. "We'll have to put our heads together and think about that later. Right now, we need to roll the trolley right into the enclosure."

Grandma held the door open, while Abbie pulled and Max pushed.

"Now Max, we'll do what we did before. We'll untie the rope and lift the canvas away from one end of the trap."

When this was done, Max remembered something important. "Abbie, we need to fill the water container. Solo may not have had a drink in ages. And what about food?"

"Good thinking, Max. You take care of the water. I keep a small mixture of food on hand for meat-eating guests. I'll put some out for Solo . . .

although I suspect he'll be too jittery to get to it tonight."

When the water and the food had been supplied, Abbie instructed Max, David and Grandma to leave the enclosure. "I'm going to open the trap door. I'm sure Solo won't rush out. He'll be too nervous. In fact, it may be hours before he feels safe enough to take a look around," Abbie explained. "And even if he did come out right away, he almost certainly wouldn't hurt us. But he *is* frightened, very frightened, and when wild animals are frightened, they are unpredictable." Abbie gestured toward the enclosure door. "So it's safer if you are all out there, and as soon as I open the trap door, I'll join you."

Max, David and Grandma did as Abbie suggested. Then they watched intently as Abbie reached down and unlocked the trap door. She lifted it up and latched it. Now Solo was free to come out whenever he wanted to.

Abbie hurried out of the enclosure and closed and locked the door. The beam from David's flashlight still shone toward the trap. There was no sign of movement.

Max pictured Solo still huddled at the back of the cage. What would it be like for him when he finally came out? What would it be like when he found not freedom, but more wire walls?

"OK, time to go home," Grandma said gently. "Your mother and father were expecting us for dinner a while ago," she reminded her grandchildren.

Max was reluctant to leave. But she knew there was nothing more they could do here for Solo. She felt tears come to her eyes, but she brushed them away. She straightened her shoulders.

Max made up her mind. She would call Sarah as soon as she could. They would get right to work on her plan for protecting wolves. And she would also try to find a way to help Solo reunite with his family, as quickly as possible.

Chapter Five

Where is Solo?

"You *have* to come," Max insisted. She looked Sarah right in the eye. "You *have* to come and meet Solo."

It was Sunday morning. Max had phoned Sarah right after dinner the night before. She had described everything that had happened – the pick-up truck arriving, the uncovering of the trap, the note and Solo's release into the enclosure. She had asked Sarah over to her house the next morning.

"Sarah, you have to come to Wild Paws with me and see this wolf *today*," Max insisted.

Sarah didn't say anything. She just twisted the end of her braid.

But Max wasn't about to give up. "Abbie said that lots of people have the wrong idea about wolves. Wolves don't hurt people. They try to stay away from people. And look." Max handed Sarah several pieces of paper. "Last night I found some information about wolves." Max pointed to a map. "They used to live all over the northern parts of the world – across nearly all of North America, Europe and Asia. Now there are far less wolves, and they're only found in parts of North America, Eastern Europe and China."

Max showed Sarah a photo that she had print-ed from her computer. A beautiful wolf with long white fur was running across a snowy plain. "Wolves are really amazing animals! They live in many different habitats. They live in the tundra of the north. They can live in forests, swamps, moun-tains and grasslands." She grinned. "I read that they baby-sit each other's pups. They're very loyal to the members of their pack. And they have amazing hearing. They can hear a mouse squeaking under a snowbank, and they can hear one another howling from three or four miles away!"

Sarah held out one of the printouts that Max had given her. "But look at this!" she said. "It gives me the shivers!" It was a photo of a wolf showing its teeth. It was standing over a dead deer.

"Well, wolves do have to eat, just like any other animal," Max said matter-of-factly. "And I read that they usually don't kill more than they can eat." She looked her friend in the eye again. "So what do you think?"

"I don't know . . . " Sarah said. "Couldn't we at least wait until after Tuesday – after Halloween night?"

"No," Max said. "Definitely not. We have a lot of work to do before then."

"What do you mean?" Sarah asked. She stopped twirling her braid and looked at Max directly.

"Listen," Max said. She poked her friend in the shoulder. "You come and see Solo with me today. Once you see him, you'll realize wolves aren't good or bad. They are just animals, wild animals, like all the other ones you love." She smiled. "And *then* I'll tell you my plan."

Sarah thought about it for a moment longer. Then she nodded. "OK, Max," she agreed. "Let's go."

Only half an hour later, Max and Sarah, bundled up in their warm jackets, were walking up the driveway to the Wild Paws and Claws Clinic and Rehabilitation Centre. They went directly to the office to say hello to Abbie.

"I'm going to take Sarah to see Solo," explained Max. "But don't worry. I remember what you said about not exposing him to humans too much. We won't get too close." Then she asked, "Has Solo come out of the trap yet this morning?"

"No, I don't think so," Abbie said. "None of his water or his food has been touched." She sighed. "It's no wonder. He *is* a wild animal, after all, and these surroundings are frightening to him." Abbie craned her neck forward and she fixed her steady gaze on Max. "But he does need to drink and eat. Stay back, but *do* take a look and see if there's any change. Oh, and Max, perhaps you and Sarah could put up the keep-out rope that we talked about. I left it outside the front door."

"Sure," Max agreed.

"And please come and report back to me after you see Solo," Abbie finished.

Max and Sarah hurried back outside. Max found the heavy rope and slung it over her shoulder. A gust of wind twirled colourful leaves across the yard.

"It's this way," said Max. She retraced the steps they had walked the night before. It didn't seem nearly as far now, in the daylight.

As soon as they got close enough to see the pen,

Max began looking for signs of the young wolf. He wasn't in the open area. She looked along the edges of the enclosure. No Solo. She searched the logs that were piled in one corner and the rocky mound that was at the other end. She looked over the raised wooden structure – a platform with a ramp and uneven walls – that was off to one side. No Solo.

"Is that the trap? Is he still inside there?" Sarah asked. Her voice trembled.

Max looked over her shoulder and saw that Sarah was hanging back. Her hands were jammed in her jacket pockets and her shoulders were hunched.

"That's it," Max said. The trap was where they had left it. The canvas still covered most of it, so it was impossible to see inside. "Here, let's tie this rope there – and there," Max decided, pointing to two trees. "It'll help give Solo privacy."

The girls quickly roped off a large area in front of Solo's enclosure.

"That's for the public. *We* have to go a little closer now, to check if Solo has had anything to drink," Max reminded Sarah.

But Sarah didn't budge. She twirled her braid nervously. "Maybe we should go and come back later," she suggested.

Max walked over to stand beside her. She put a hand on Sarah's arm. "How about I go and check Solo's food and water? Why don't you sit here and wait for me?" she offered, pointing to a nearby bench. "I'll be right back."

Sarah looked grateful as she sat down.

Max headed straight over to the pen. She took a quick look inside the water container and glanced at the food bin. Solo was nowhere in sight.

She returned and dropped down on the bench beside Sarah. "The water container looks just as full as it did last night when I put the water in," Max said. "And he still hasn't touched the food. Sarah, I'm worried about Solo. Let's sit here for a bit and see if he comes out."

Solo's pen was at the very far edge of the enclosure area. From where they sat, Sarah and Max could see Bandit's hollow tree and Flora's den.

Ch-ch-ch-ch.

They could hear Nutcracker scolding some unfortunate passerby – a bird or a wild squirrel. They could see Tippy, the red fox, as he moved about his pen. He only had three black-stockinged legs, but he moved easily, hopping a little with his back leg. He held his bushy tail straight out, the white fur on the end of it flicking like a flag.

Max and Sarah sat quietly. Gradually, Max could feel Sarah relax. It was peaceful here. The air was cool, but the sun was shining down on them. It warmed the tops of their heads and made the colours in the leaves seem more vibrant.

Max sighed. She loved sitting with the animals at Wild Paws and Claws. It felt like home. She closed her eyes for a moment and turned her face up to the sun.

Suddenly, she heard Sarah draw in a sharp breath. Max's eyes flew open. She smiled. A black nose had appeared at the end of the trap, and it was sniffing the air!

Chapter Six

How Can We Help?

"Shh," Max warned Sarah, her finger to her mouth.

She snuck a look at her friend. Sarah's face was tense and her lips were pressed tightly together. She looked like she wanted to run away.

"Don't move," Max begged her in a whisper. "We'll just sit here and watch."

Sarah didn't agree, but she didn't try to leave.

Now Max turned her attention back to the trap. Yes, there was Solo's black nose, and now she could see his long muzzle and now his whole head. Max smiled. The young wolf was beautiful. He looked this way and that, with watchful eyes.

His big ears were pricked forward, twisting and turning.

Ch-ch-ch-ch.

Solo turned toward the noisy squirrel and cocked his head to one side. Max had to stifle a giggle.

Solo seemed to quickly decide that Nutcracker was nothing to worry about. Then he focused his attention on the water and food, which were waiting for him near the logs. He took one dainty step forward and then another.

Now Sarah breathed out in a long, admiring "Ohhhhh." Max glanced at her. When she saw the beginnings of a smile on Sarah's face, she knew everything was going to be OK.

Solo continued to step slowly across the open area, toward the water container. He seemed alert to every sound and smell. He looked ready to dash back to the trap at the slightest hint of danger. When he reached the water, he glanced around for a few minutes before finally lowering his head to drink. He lapped greedily at the liquid.

Then he paused, lifted his head and surveyed the area again.

Ch-ch-ch-ch.

This time, Solo didn't even look in the nagging

squirrel's direction. He dropped his head again, and now he ate the food, gulping it down in several large bites.

Max and Sarah looked with wide eyes as Solo finally seemed to relax. Now that he wasn't thirsty or hungry, he slowly walked around the edge of his enclosure. He sniffed here and there. He was watchful, but no longer nervous. Max thought he might return to the trap – the place that he knew – but he didn't. Instead, he picked out a protected spot at the edge of some brush near the rocky mound. He pawed at the leaves, circled a few times and then curled up into a tight ball.

Max and Sarah slowly exhaled. They had been so interested in watching Solo explore his surroundings that they had forgotten to breathe.

"What do you think about wolves now?" Max said softly, looking into her friend's kind blue eyes.

"I think . . . " Sarah paused. "Well, I think you were right. I needed to see a real wolf." She shook her head in amazement. "Solo is beautiful. He's . . . beautiful. He isn't good or bad. He's just . . . wild." Sarah grinned at Max. "I guess wolves are OK after all."

Then her curiosity got the better of her. "Now

quick, Max, tell me your plan. How can we help the wolves?"

Max explained her idea to Sarah. A broad grin spread across Sarah's face. "It's great!" she exclaimed. "Let's go talk to Abbie!"

Abbie was sitting behind her desk in her office. As always, it was piled high with papers to be filed and forms to be filled in. A dirty teacup balanced atop a stack of books about wild animals.

"You see, it's just perfect timing," Max explained. "Halloween is only two days away! It's ideal!"

"It'll make it so easy to get people here," said Sarah.

"And then once they're here . . . " began Max.

"We're all set!" finished Sarah.

"I *know* all the kids at our school will come," Max promised.

Abbie's round glasses sat at the very tip of her thin nose. Her head swung back and forth as she listened to first Max, then Sarah, then Max again and Sarah again . . . "Whoa, slow down, slow down," she finally begged, hooting with laughter. "You have to start again! Sit down, both of you, and start again at the beginning."

Max and Sarah were bubbling over with

excitement, but they both found a place to sit.✳
Max took a tray of old birds' nests off a chair and
set it gently on the windowsill. Sarah perched on
the edge of a stool that held a mountain of old
magazines.

"We want people to stop being afraid of wolves.
We want people to stop hurting them. Plus, we
want Solo to return to his pack." Max looked at
Abbie, who nodded in agreement. "So we need to
have a Halloween party here on Halloween night,"
Max stated.

Abbie's eyebrows shot up, but she didn't say a
word.

Sarah took over explaining. "We're going to
make flyers today and hand them out at school
tomorrow. We'll ask the students to take a bunch
home and give them to people on Halloween,
when they're trick-or-treating."

"The flyers will have information about wolves
on one side. We can include some of the facts that
I already researched on the Internet," Max said.
"And I know that you have lots of great books
about animals here, Abbie. We can look through
them to find more interesting details about
wolves."

Sarah's eyes lit up. "On the other side of the

flyer will be an invitation: *Please come to a costume party at Wild Paws and Claws, after trick-or-treating!* " She clapped her hands together. "Maybe we could set up some games and have some treats. We'll have a fun presentation on wolves, and people can have a look at Solo — from a distance, of course."

"They won't be able to see him too well," Max worried aloud.

"No, they won't," Abbie agreed. She tapped her finger on her chin thoughtfully.

"You know what? I have an idea. Sometimes when I needed to keep watch on one of my animals in an outdoor pen, I would set up my video camera there. This was before I had dedicated helpers, of course," she added with a wink. "I'd hook it up to the TV in the main office, and then I could keep an eye on things all day long."

"That's a great idea!" Max cried. "We can film Solo without disturbing him, and our visitors can watch him live and up close on television."

"Right," agreed Abbie. "That way they'll get a good chance to see how special he is."

Chapter Seven

Making Plans

Abbie craned her neck forward. She peered over her glasses at Max and then at Sarah. Then she smiled. "Well girls, you've done it again. You've come up with another great idea!"

Max laughed with relief. Her feeling of helplessness began to disappear. They could do something to try to help the local wolf pack and Solo!

Max wanted to get busy right away. But first they had to decide on what there was to do — and who would do it.

"It's important that we hand out the party flyers tomorrow," Max said, thinking aloud.

Sarah nodded. "Yes. That gives everyone lots of

time to plan to come here on Halloween night. You and I should work on that first, Max."

"Right," Max agreed. She had some other suggestions too. All the night before, she had thought about ways to encourage people to come to this event. If more people came, more people would learn about wolves.

"We need some games and decorations and treats for our event," she went on. But Max knew that Wild Paws and Claws didn't have much money. There was just enough to buy food and supplies for the animals . . . for now. "Abbie, could you try to arrange for some donations for our party? Mr. Lee runs the fruit store, and his daughter, Elizabeth, is in our class at school. Mr. Lee and Elizabeth came to our open house here. Maybe he could donate some apples for apple bobbing."

"All right," said Abbie, writing down the suggestion.

"It would be fun to have a costume contest," piped up Sarah. "Maybe we could have a prize for the scariest one."

"And one for the funniest," suggested Abbie.

"I know!" added Max. "We could have a prize for the best wolf costume too! We can put that on our flyer."

Abbie and Sarah excitedly agreed.

"But what about decorations?" Max asked. "We need to make lots. And we need treats too — for the little kids." Then Max snapped her fingers. "Abbie, do you think you could call Ms Fennario, who owns the party store in town? Could you ask her for a donation of decorations and treats?"

"Certainly," Abbie agreed. "Ms Fennario is a very kind woman. She once brought an injured squirrel to Wild Paws and Claws. She may be able to help out." Abbie nodded her head as she wrote down another note to herself.

Max smiled. She felt excited about planning the event. But she felt nervous too. There was so much to be done!

"Abbie, we'll do the chores for you today, while you make those phone calls. Let's go, Sarah. We'll get them done quickly so we can get to work writing the flyer," Max suggested.

The two helpers divided up the jobs and hurried outside. Max went to the Bird Trail, the little path that circled through the woods behind the animal pens. It had some swallow houses and several bird feeders. Max filled a bucket and walked along the trail, topping up the feeders with new seed.

There were many signs at the centre to help

guide visitors to places of interest. *This way to the raptor pens. This way to the raccoons.* Sarah took a paintbrush and a small can of black paint. She walked around the centre, checking each sign and touching up any words that needed some fresh paint.

Then the girls put on their work gloves and they went on their rounds to give the animals fresh water.

"How about I take care of the birds, and you do the other animals?" Max suggested.

"Sure," Sarah agreed.

Abbie had made a panel in the mesh of each creature's pen. The panel was on a hinge so that it could swing open. Max visited Clarice, the great horned owl, first. Clarice sat on her high perch, sound asleep, her back to Max. Max reached in, took out the owl's water container and emptied out what was left over. Then she refilled it with fresh water, replaced it in the pen and closed the panel.

Next Max visited Feathers, the red-tailed hawk. The stocky raptor was alert. He was perched on a tree within his pen.

Keeeer-r-r, keeeer-r-r, cried Feathers, ruffling his feathers and wagging his tail at the disturbance.

"Yes, yes," agreed Max, reaching into the pen for Feathers' water container. "I know you'd rather be left alone, but then you'd be awfully thirsty later!"

Soon Max had finished. She hurried back to the yard and joined Sarah in putting the water buckets, scoops and gloves away in the storage shed. Then the girls cheerfully burst into the office building. Abbie was sitting behind her desk, speaking on the telephone. She waved at the girls and kept talking.

Max settled in front of the computer and Sarah headed for the bookshelves. They worked steadily for several hours. Every now and then they would stop to discuss the facts they were discovering about wolves. There was so much to tell that the girls could hardly decide what to include in the flyer and what to leave out.

They were surprised when Abbie interrupted them. "It's almost two o'clock. Eat your lunches!" she reminded the girls. "Aren't you starving?"

Max had been ignoring her grumbling stomach. She didn't want to lose any time on their project. They only had two days to make the flyers and give them out, to plan a party and, most importantly, to come up with a great presentation on wolves. Max swallowed hard. "We can eat while we work," she suggested to Sarah, who agreed.

But Max couldn't even eat one bite of her lunch. Her stomach was empty, but it was in knots. Would their plan to save the wolves succeed — or fail?

Chapter Eight

Chipping In

Max's spirits lifted when she heard Abbie's news.

"Girls, guess what?" Abbie announced, setting down the telephone receiver. "Ken Lee has agreed to donate three bushels of apples for our apple-bobbing. Laura Fennario is setting aside four large bags of candy, some Halloween decorations and craft supplies in Halloween colours. Plus, I called a trophy store in the city. The manager has agreed to give us three trophies to hand out for the costume contest!"

"Hurray!" Max cheered. "Everyone's chipping in!"

A little while later, Max and Sarah were almost

finished their final draft of the handout. On one side, there was a cheerful invitation: *Come to a costume party at Wild Paws and Claws, at seven o'clock on Halloween night. There will be games and treats. Win a prize for the scariest costume, the funniest costume or the most realistic wolf costume. Meet Solo, a special Halloween guest!* On the other side was terrific information about wolves.

"We're missing one thing, though," said Max thoughtfully.

Sarah's blue eyes looked concerned. "What's that?"

"We need to add a message. To the people who saved Solo from the trap," Max replied. "One of them was a girl dressed in a vampire costume. She probably goes to our school! We need to convince her to come to the party — or at least to tell us, somehow, where she found Solo."

"How can we do that?" Sarah asked.

"Let's see," Max pondered. "We have to word it so only *she* will know what we mean. We don't want to scare her off."

Thrum, thrum, thrum. Max tapped her fingers on the tabletop. Suddenly she snapped them and said, "What about saying something like, 'Were you the one who delivered the package to Wild Paws and

Claws on Saturday night? Good work. It arrived safely.' "

"That's good," said Sarah. "Go on. See if you can find a way to ask where Solo came from."

"Hmm . . . " Max thought some more. "How about this? 'But the contents need to be returned to where they came from. Please come and see us, or call with directions.' "

"Perfect!" Sarah cried, looking proudly at her friend. Quickly she keyed the words into the computer. Then she ran off the new version of the flyer.

"Now all we need to do is make copies of this," Sarah said. "Lots of copies."

"And we're going to do that right now," Abbie said, poking her head around the doorway. "I'll drop you at the copy place while I pick up all the donations. Samantha Ali said she'd let you run off enough flyers to give some to each student at your school!"

It was getting dark by the time they'd finished in town. Abbie dropped off Sarah at her house. "Bye, Sarah," called Max. "Don't forget. Meet me early at school so we can get permission to give out our flyers!"

"You bet," promised Sarah.

Next Abbie dropped off Max. "Sarah and I will

come to Wild Paws right after school tomorrow," Max assured her. "We've got a lot to do. We have to clean out the tubs for apple bobbing. We have to put up the decorations and make some new ones." She counted off all the jobs on her fingers. "We have to work on our wolf presentation. And, most important of all," Max said, looking up at Abbie with a grin, "we have to visit Solo and see how he's doing."

Then the smile faded from Max's face. She was picturing the young wolf, huddled in the corner of the trap, scared and uncertain. "Oh, Abbie, I like Solo a lot. But I hope he'll be going home soon."

"Me too," said Abbie. "It would certainly be best for him."

"But what if we can't find his pack?" Max asked, her voice shaky. "When I was reading about wolves, I learned that autumn is their favourite season. They sometimes travel around their whole territory then. Some scientists think the adults are showing the young wolves the boundaries of their home." Max felt her eyes getting damp with tears, and she rubbed at them briskly. "What if that's what was happening when Solo got trapped – and the pack has gone on without him? We might *never* find them!" Max swallowed hard. "The size of a wolf pack's territory can be between one hundred and *three thousand* square kilometres. That's a huge amount of space!"

Abbie patted her on the shoulder. "Max, calm down," she said gently. "I know you're worried, but you're doing all you can for Solo. Let's wait and see what happens after your notice goes out. Maybe we'll find some answers from the young people who brought that little fellow to us." She peered intently at Max through her glasses. "If not, I'm sure we'll come up with another plan. You and Sarah and I will just have to put our heads together."

Max nodded. She thought about the great flyers she was holding in her lap. She thought about their secret message. It just *had* to work!

"Now off you go for dinner. You've worked hard today. Have a nice relaxing evening," Abbie told her.

"Good night, Abbie," Max replied, sliding out of the station wagon with her load of flyers. Abbie was right. She should stop worrying – and she knew just what would help her do that.

She called hello to her family, who were already gathering at the dinner table. "I'll be there in just a minute!" she added. Max picked up the telephone and dialled Sarah's number.

"Could you come over after dinner?" she asked Sarah. "I don't want to wait till tomorrow to start planning our presentation. If we start tonight, we can make it extra special!"

Max waited for Sarah's response. She didn't want her to say no.

When Max replaced the receiver, she was smiling again. Sarah had agreed right away. Max was so lucky to have such a great friend — a friend who loved animals as much as she; a friend who loved wolves!

Chapter Nine

Halloween Party

"It's Halloween! It's Halloween! It's Halloween!" David was dancing around the house in his wolf costume, flapping his huge claws and singing.

"Max, are you sure you don't want to go trick-or-treating with your brother for even a little while?" her mother asked.

"I don't have time, Mom," Max replied cheerfully. "But it's OK. I'll get some treats at Wild Paws and Claws." She slipped on her mask and began buckling up her belt. A long, bushy black tail dangled from it.

Max had decided to wear a wolf costume too, in honour of Solo. All the wolf masks in town were the same – angry and snarling. So Max had made her own. She had been busy at Wild Paws yesterday after school, continuing to prepare for tonight's event. She and Sarah had put the finishing touches on their wolf presentation and they had made more Halloween decorations.

But she had also found some time to spend with Solo. She had sat quietly behind the keep-out rope and gazed at the beautiful wolf. She had watched as he explored the inside of the enclosure. He moved so smoothly, like an athlete! Solo had kept glancing in her direction, his ears tilting, always alert.

"It's OK, Solo," she had whispered to him, even though he couldn't hear her words. "We'll get you back to your family."

Max had examined Solo's pointy ears, his yellow eyes, his long, narrow muzzle and the fluffy fur that surrounded his face, making it seem wide. She had made a pencil sketch of his face. Then last night, she had used cardboard, paper, tape, wool and an old hat to make a wolf mask. She thought it looked pretty realistic – more so than a store-bought one, anyway!

Max tightened her belt and hurried downstairs. She was just reaching for her jacket when Sarah knocked on the front door. Max said hi to Sarah

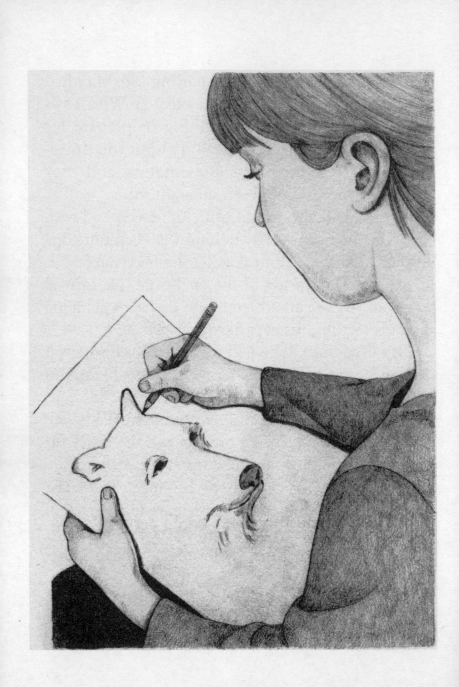

and called over her shoulder, "Bye, everyone!"

Grandma was in the kitchen preparing coins for the trick-or-treaters' UNICEF boxes. "See you at Wild Paws," she called back. "We'll all meet you there around seven o'clock!"

The time passed quickly.

At the wildlife centre, Max and Sarah hurried to put the final touches on the party. First they turned on some of the outdoor lights. They had draped strings of orange and red bulbs through some of the trees. Those helped to set a spooky mood.

Max's dad had lent his CD player and speakers to Wild Paws and Claws for the evening, along with several Halloween CDs. Now the air was filled with haunted sounds.

Earlier, Abbie and the girls had set up the video camera near Solo's pen and run a cord to the main building. When they switched on the office TV, it worked beautifully. They could see Solo sleeping in the protected spot near the rocky mound.

Abbie had set up tables in the yard. She'd put a bushel of apples on one, and set a bucket of water next to it. Max helped her fill a second bucket. "I hope there'll be time to have a look at Solo before anyone arrives tonight," she told Abbie. "I want to see how he's doing."

"He ate this morning," Abbie reassured her.

Max nodded, but she knew the news was good and not so good. It was good because it meant Solo wasn't going to starve. But it was not so good if it meant that Solo was getting used to being captive. The longer he stayed in the enclosure, being looked after by people, the tougher it would be for him to rejoin his pack.

"How many apples should go in each bucket?" Sarah asked. "Four?" She dropped four apples in each one. "I think we're going to need paper towels so that the apple bobbers can dry off afterwards."

"Good idea," agreed Max, and she hurried to get some.

Max and Sarah had planned a scavenger hunt with clues, and they checked to make sure that the first clues were ready in a bowl. They decided to display the three best-costume trophies on one of the outdoor tables. Then they finished preparing the candy treats for the guests and put them on one of the outdoor tables too.

"The place looks great!"

"Terrific!" Grandma, Dad, Mom and David had arrived. They admired the tissue-paper witch and ghost decorations that swayed gently in the evening breeze.

Max felt her stomach twist nervously. They had given out all the flyers at school. All the kids had been excited about the party. Many of them had taken extra flyers to hand out as they were trick-or-treating. Max was sure that the kid who had rescued Solo *must* have read the flyer – and the secret message.

Max had checked at the office for phone messages: nothing. So far, there hadn't been a phone call to Wild Paws and Claws telling them where the trap had been found.

It's OK. There's still tonight. The two rescuers will come to the party. They'll tell us here, Max told herself firmly.

"Come on, Max." Sarah was tugging on her sleeve. Several cars had arrived in the parking lot. Many people were walking down the long laneway to the clinic. "The party's starting!"

The event began really well. Wolves, skeletons, Frankenstein monsters and trolls lined up for apple bobbing. The scavenger hunt sent ghosts, witches, pirates and fairies searching for clues. Parents and kids snacked on chips and Dracula Dip, munched Goblin Cookies and Eyeball Delights and sipped Swamp-Monster Punch.

Max was enjoying herself. But there were only

two vampires at the Halloween party, and Max recognised them both. They were grade-six kids from her school. They were too big to be the little vampire who had brought Solo on Saturday night.

Next came the costume contest. Abbie was the judge. She stood in the middle of the yard, peering intently at each outfit as the trick-or-treaters paraded around her in a circle. When she chose the winners and presented the trophies, everyone clapped.

"This is the time that we chose for our wolf talk," Sarah reminded Max.

"You're right." The girls paused and looked at each other. They were both nervous. Max didn't like speaking in front of an audience. But she knew she had to do it. They both had to do it, for Solo and all the other wolves.

Max and Sarah stood in front of the crowd and introduced their talk. They pointed to all the kids who had dressed in wolf costumes, and they described what real wolves looked like. They talked about the habits of wolves. They explained that healthy wild wolves hardly ever attacked farm animals, and that they never hurt people. Sarah said that she had once been afraid of wolves, and she told everyone why she wasn't afraid anymore.

"And now," Max said, "we'd like you to meet a wolf."

All the trick-or-treaters became absolutely silent.

"A young wolf, whom we have named Solo, was brought to Wild Paws and Claws three nights ago. We think a wolf pack has returned to the Maple Hill area. And we think that Solo is from this local wolf pack."

Max heard several children gasp, and her heart sank. They were still nervous about wolves, even after the presentation. Then she remembered that Sarah had been afraid too, until she had met Solo. Solo would just have to do it again. He would have to do what Max and Sarah couldn't do — convince people that he was a special animal who deserved to run free.

"You won't be able to see Solo in his pen. Instead, we'll have a quick tour of the other animals and then return to the office, where you can see Solo — live — on the television there. We don't want you getting too close to Solo. It's not because he's dangerous," Max added quickly. "It's because we don't want him to get used to people. We want him to remain a wild wolf!"

Sarah and Abbie each held a large flashlight. Max carried Abbie's special night-vision light.

"Please follow us," Max instructed the guests to Wild Paws and Claws. "We'll have a quick look at some of the other animals who live here. Don't be surprised if some of them are asleep! Then we'll show you Solo."

Max and Sarah began leading the large group of visitors down the path to the enclosures. They could faintly hear the spooky music, with its howls, screeches and groans. The flashlight beams made the shadows dart and dance, and Max noticed some of the tinier ghosts and goblins reaching for their parents' hands.

Nutcracker the squirrel and Tippy the fox were asleep, curled up in their pens. But Max whispered softly to each of them anyway: "Happy Halloween."

Bandit and Flora were active and alert. Bandit skilfully tight-roped across one of the narrow, high rails in the pen. Flora soon followed him. "They've probably never had visitors at night before," grinned Sarah in the dark.

When they reached the end of the enclosures, they came to the rope that Sarah and Max had used to prevent visitors from coming too close.

"I'll stay here and shine my flashlight near Solo so that everyone can see him on the television," said Max.

"Okay," Sarah and Abbie agreed. The two of them instructed the guests to head toward the office.

Max waited as they moved away. She enjoyed the silence of the evening as the last of the chattering ghosts and goblins disappeared out of sight. She looked toward Solo's pen, anxious to see the young wolf, but not wanting to get too close to him until she was certain everyone was gathered in front of the television.

After about five minutes had passed, Max felt confident that the time was right. She shone the beam of her night-vision flashlight near Solo. The red light would let the visitors see him clearly, but it wouldn't bother Solo like a regular flashlight would.

The young wolf was wide awake. He was pacing one way and then the other, his tail straight out behind him. He seemed excited.

Then, all of a sudden, Max jumped as a voice came out of the darkness. "I need to speak to you." Max turned, startled, and saw a little ghost standing beside her.

Chapter Ten

Aooooo!

"Oh, you surprised me!" Max told the small child. She spoke in a whisper so as not to frighten Solo. "But you shouldn't be here. You should have gone with the others to watch the wolf on the TV."

But the ghost didn't move. "But I needed to speak to you," she said softly. "I've seen the wolf before," she admitted in a shaky voice.

Max's eyes widened. Suddenly she knew. The vampire hadn't come to the party tonight. Because a ghost had come instead. "Listen," she said urgently. She stared into the ghost's eyes. "You have to tell me. Where did you find Solo? Where?"

For a moment, the ghost didn't speak.

Then suddenly the silence was filled with the most amazing sound. It was spine-tingling. It was haunting. It was sad and mournful and wonderful.

Aooooo!

It was the howl of a wolf.

Max was stunned. The howl sounded so real. But it couldn't be. Could it? No, it's just the Halloween recording, she thought. It's full of howls and other spooky sounds. Someone must have turned it up louder. That had to be it. What other explanation could there be?

Max turned back to the ghost. She still needed information from her.

But again the magical sound filled the air.

Aooooo!

The cry was high. It rose sharply, then slid down in ripples, like waves. Max felt herself shiver. Now she knew for certain. This couldn't be a recording.

Aooooo! Aooooo!

The first howl was joined by a second howl. And then a third.

It was almost impossible to tell where the sounds were coming from. Max looked at Solo – he wasn't howling. The cries seemed to wrap around Max, filling the dark night with their wonderful longing.

Max was bursting with excitement. Wild wolves howling! She had never heard this strange, wailing cry before.

Then Max felt a tug on her arm. "Why are they howling?" It was the little ghost speaking.

"There could be lots of reasons," Max told her. "Often a pack will howl to tell other wolves about its location. It warns them to stay out of its territory. Wolves might also howl to call the pack together before a hunt. Or they might howl to find one another if they are separated, say, during a snowstorm."

The beam of Max's flashlight still bathed the young wolf. Now he stood with his tail between his back legs. He lifted his head into the air, put his ears back and pointed his black nose at the sky.

Aooooo! Aooooo!

Solo was answering back! His mouth was wide and his eyes seemed almost to close as he sang.

Aooooo!

"The wolves have found each other!" Max said to the little ghost. "It's incredible!"

"Where are they? Where's the wolf pack?"

"It's hard to know," Max explained. "The sound of wolves howling can travel for nearly ten kilometres! The pack could be close by — or very far away."

Max looked toward Solo. "Solo was separated from his pack when he got caught in that trap you found," she told the ghost. "You were going to tell me where you found him."

The ghost didn't speak. Instead, she gave a quick nod.

"Thank you," Max said. "You and your brother were very brave and kind to bring Solo here to the clinic. You two were the first to rescue him. Now Solo's pack has come to finish your great work."

Max grinned and the ghost smiled cheerfully back at her, her brown eyes glowing through the holes cut into the white sheet.

Aooooo! Aooooo!

Max listened as the pack howled again. The sound rose and then fell, slowly dropping away.

But this time . . . something seemed different.

The smile on Max's face froze. It seemed that the howling was fainter. Was it just that fewer wolves were howling? Or was the wolf pack moving away?

Were the wolves leaving Solo behind?

Chapter Eleven

No Time to Waste

Max's sense of relief vanished. She knew she had to do something . . . *fast*. She knew Solo had to go free.

"Listen," she told the little ghost urgently. "We have to get back to the office. We have to find Abbie."

But just then, Abbie was there, hurrying down the path toward Max, the beam of her flashlight bobbing ahead of her. Of course, Max realized. Abbie had been watching. She had seen – and heard – what was happening. Everyone had!

"Abbie, we have to release Solo," she began.

But Abbie was already nodding her head. "Yes,

Max, you're right. There's no time to waste." Her words were brisk and firm. "This little ghost will stick near me. You open the enclosure door and let Solo out."

"All right," Max said.

Aooooo! Aooooo!

It was the wolf pack. The wolves hadn't given up. They were calling again.

Max's heart started pounding harder. It wasn't too late! *It wasn't too late!*

But she didn't want to take any chances. She moved quickly toward the door of Solo's enclosure. Max saw Solo lower his head. She saw him turn. Briefly, he looked at Abbie and the little ghost. Then Solo looked right at Max.

Max remembered seeing Solo for the first time, just four days ago. David had thought that Solo looked like a German shepherd dog. And she had almost thought so too. Now, after spending so much time watching Solo, she felt she knew the young wolf very well. She knew she could picture him in her sleep — his wide paws, his long tan and brown fur, the curious expression on his face, the way he cocked his head to one side when he listened to Nutcracker.

"Your family is waiting for you, Solo," Max told

him. "They haven't forgotten you. And I won't, either."

Max unlocked the door to Solo's enclosure. She opened it wide. Then she turned and walked briskly back to where the others stood, behind the keep-out rope. Max turned off her flashlight. She, Abbie and the little ghost waited silently.

And all of a sudden, the sky became bright. The clouds shifted for a moment and the moon shone through.

Max could see Solo, still standing, looking toward her.

And then came another howl: *Aooooo! Aooooo!*

Solo took a step, and then he hesitated.

"Go, Solo. Go on," Max whispered intently to the wolf. She clenched her hands nervously. "Get out of there. Go and join your family."

One long moment stretched into the next one. Then, slowly, Solo took another step and then another. He moved past the trap without glancing at it. Step by step, he moved toward the open door.

Max held her breath. She didn't dare even whisper now.

Go on. Go on, Solo.

For another long moment, Solo stood at the

door to the pen. He was surrounded by fences of steel, a prisoner.

Did he look at Max one more time? She thought so, but she wasn't sure.

And then suddenly, the young wolf sprang forward and through the door. Before Max could blink, just as the clouds moved back in front of the moon, Solo chose freedom — and was gone.

Chapter Twelve

One Final Problem

Max, Abbie and the little ghost walked up the path toward the office. When they reached it, Max was surprised to find that the large group of Halloween guests was still there. They had been waiting for them to return.

A little skeleton and a larger robot ran up to her. "What happened? What happened?" they asked.

Soon everyone was crowding around Max.

"Did the young wolf get back to his family?" asked a woman who had a bundled-up baby in her arms and a small witch at her side.

"Is everything all right now?" inquired a grey-haired man. "I grew up north of here. There was a wolf pack around years ago. It never caused anyone any harm. Wolves need someplace to live too, you know." He scratched his chin vigorously. "That's what I've always thought, anyway."

A little cowboy chimed in, "The wolf wasn't scary. I like wolves."

Then Sarah and Abbie were at Max's side. Abbie put up her hand and called for quiet. Everyone looked intently at Max. "Solo is gone," she said simply. "He went to join his family."

"Hurray," called out several people, and others clapped.

"And now the party is officially over," Abbie announced. She grinned. "Don't forget to help yourselves to some candy before you leave," she told the trick-or-treaters.

Sarah and Max gave out the treats. And one by one and two by two, the ghouls, goblins, fairies and black cats said thank you and goodbye.

The last two people to leave were a walking pumpkin and her father. After the pumpkin accepted some candy and said goodbye, her father nodded seriously at Max. "Great presentation. We'll have to have a talk with one of our neighbours . . . about his traps."

Finally, only Abbie, Sarah and her mother and

Max and her family were left. The night was quiet. The Halloween CD had been replayed twice and had ended for the last time several minutes ago.

The group put away the tables and the barrels. Abbie put the leftover apples in the shed. "Bandit and Flora will enjoy these!" she said to Max, grinning. Then she yawned. "It's time to go home. I'll take down the decorations in the morning."

Abbie put one skinny arm around Sarah and one around Max. "Good work, you two," she congratulated them. "You gave a fun party, you helped many people learn about wolves and . . . Solo is back with his pack!"

Max felt a warm glow of happiness.

"I think we really *did* help some people get over their fear of wolves," Max agreed. "And I'm happy Solo is with his family." She pictured the pup standing at the door of the pen — and then running free. She imagined him finding his family in the forest. She could almost see the moonlight shining down on them, the wolves meeting Solo with happy nuzzling and tail wagging. "But that had nothing to do with Sarah and me. Solo's pack came looking for him all on their own." Max added, "The little vampire came tonight dressed as a ghost. She had read our flyer, and she was going to tell us where she found the trap. But she didn't need to. Solo's family came to rescue him themselves!"

"Ah, but Max," Abbie said, squeezing Max's shoulder, "on any normal night, the pack might have come and howled. And Solo might have howled back. But there would have been no one around to hear the wolves. There would have been no one here to realize that the pack was searching for its missing wolf. There would have been no one here to release Solo."

Maybe Abbie was right. Sarah and Max looked at each other and grinned. It felt good to know that Solo was free. And it felt good to know that they had helped make it happen.

"OK, enough of this talk about wolves," Grandma called, a smile in her voice. She began heading to the parking lot. "Let's go home. I want to see what kind of candies I got in my grab bag."

Everyone laughed. Abbie said good night and went to turn off the lights in the office. "See you Thursday after school?" she asked Max and Sarah.

"You bet," they assured her.

Then the two girls followed their parents and David to the parking lot. "It was a wonderful night," Sarah said.

"It sure was," sighed Max. She carried her wolf mask in her hand. It was time to leave Wild Paws and Claws for another day.

"There's only one final problem," Sarah added. Her voice was serious.

Max blinked. "What problem?" she asked.

"Solo's name," Sarah said. She gazed ahead as they walked.

Max stared at her friend. What was she talking about? "Why is Solo's name a problem?" she asked.

"Solo. Solo," Sarah repeated. She had been keeping her face out of view, but now Max could see that Sarah was trying not to grin. "Just think about it for a minute," she told Max.

And suddenly Max was grinning too. "I get it! I get it!" Max cried. "Solo means alone, but Solo isn't alone anymore."

Max looked out into the dark night. Somewhere out there was a wolf pack. Somewhere out there was a young wolf with long pointy ears, too-big paws and curious yellow eyes. And now he wasn't scared and uncertain and alone. He was with his family. He was home.

"You're right," Max told Sarah. "It is a problem!" Then she smiled happily. "But, oh, what a wonderful problem to have!"

Wolf Information Sheet

🐾 Wolves used to be found almost everywhere in North America. Now there are many areas on the continent without wolves. Wolves can be found in most parts of Canada, except the Atlantic provinces. They are almost extinct in the United States.

🐾 Although some wolves do live alone, most wolves live in a family or pack. A typical wolf pack is made up of two parents, four to eight pups and some close relatives (perhaps young wolves from the parents' previous litters). The male and female parents are the leaders. All the other wolves are placed, or ranked, under the leaders.

🐾 Wolves in a pack hardly ever fight among themselves. Each wolf knows its place! But occasionally one will challenge a leader or other wolves higher in rank. If a leader loses a challenge, it will sometimes leave the pack and go it alone.

🐾 Wolves can communicate a lot with their tails.
• A tail held loosely: the wolf is relaxed.

• A tail held high and curving upward: this is a threat. The wolf is ready to prove that it is dominant, or higher in rank.

• A tail tucked under: the wolf is showing that it is not a threat. It is showing that it is lower in rank.

🐾 Wolves will eat almost anything they can catch. Alone, a wolf will hunt and eat mice, squirrels, beavers, geese and sometimes fish. Wolves hunt together in packs for larger animals, such as caribou, deer, moose or bighorn sheep.

🐾 Wolves are the largest wild member of the dog family. They look a little like German shepherds, but wolves have larger heads, bushier tails, longer legs, bigger feet and different fur colouration. Adult males usually weigh between 35 and 55 kilograms. Most adult females weigh between 25 and 40 kilograms. But adult wolves can weigh anywhere from as much as a human child to as much as a human adult!